CONTENTS

1. Good, Good, Good, Good 1
   A Lesson about God's Goodness in Creation

2. Don't Eat from That Tree 3
   A Lesson about Choosing to Obey

3. They Missed the Boat 5
   A Lesson about Following God instead of the Crowd

4. Babel, Babel, Babel, Babel 7
   A Lesson about Doing God's Will

5. God Specializes in Surprises 9
   A Lesson about Trusting God to Be Good

6. Jo-Jo-Joseph Had a Rainbow Coat 11
   A Lesson about Jealousy

7. Gideon, I'm Not Kideon 13
   A Lesson about God's Strength for Tough Jobs

8. Yes! 15
   A Lesson about Listening for God

9. No Matter How Little You Are 17
   A Lesson about Being Used by God

10. Sol, Sol the Know-It-All 19
    A Lesson about Being Smart and Acting Smart

11. Shadrach, Meshach, Abednego 21
    A Lesson about Standing Up for God

12. Meow, Meow 23
    A Lesson about Doing What's Right No Matter What

13. Indigestible Jonah 25
    A Lesson about Obeying Right Away

14. Oh-Me-Ah, Oh-My-Ah 27
    A Lesson about Studying the Bible

Copyright © 2000 by Tyndale House Publishers, Inc., Wheaton, Illinois. All rights reserved.

Song lyrics copyright © 2000 Steve Siler: Manler Music/Word Music, Inc.—ASCAP; John Mandeville: Sideville Music/Dayspring Music, Inc.—BMI. Used by permission.

Executive Producers Tammy Faxel and Shawn McSpadden
Product Manager Jacki Vietmeier
Designed by Gloria Chantell
Devotions and lessons written and compiled by Erin Keeley

All Scripture quotations taken from the *Holy Bible*, New Living Translation, copyright © 1996. Used by permission of Tyndale House Publishers, Inc., Wheaton, Illinois 60189. All rights reserved.

ISBN 0-8423-5359-3

Book printed in U.S.A.

04 03 02 01 00
5   4   3   2   1

Good, Good, Good, Good

A LESSON ABOUT GOD'S GOODNESS IN CREATION

🄌 BIBLE STORY

Teacher's Note: Read the story of Creation to the class. It's found in Genesis 1:1–2:4.

❸ THE STORY IN SONG

Teacher's Note: Play the song "Good, Good, Good, Good" from Bible Songs 1.

"GOOD, GOOD, GOOD, GOOD"

(THE CREATION SONG)

On day one God made earth
Then he made the heavens
Then he said let there be light
That made night and day
On day two God made space
To separate the waters
That made sky and oceans wide
On the second day

CHORUS:
Good, good, good, good
He saw that it was very good
Good, good, good, good
God saw that it was good

On day three God made land
Fruits and plants and trees
On day four he made the stars
And the moon and sun
On day five he made fish
And the warbling birdies
So the skies were filled with song
And day five was done

REPEAT CHORUS

On day six God made cows
Bears and mice and monkeys
Animals of every kind
Creatures great and small

He made man, woman too
Then his work was finished
So on day seven God leaned back
And this is what he saw

REPEAT CHORUS

❷ DIGGING DEEPER DEVOTION

Teacher's Note: Read the following devotion to the children and discuss the questions that come after it.

Back when God created everything, he made the earth with just enough water in the seas, just enough warmth in the sun, and just the right foods to meet our needs. Think of the variety of beautiful flowers, amazing animals, sparkling stars, and glorious colors. God is very creative! He did everything well—right down to the order of things. Did you know he waited to create humans until the earth had everything we needed to survive? It was perfect! What a good, good, good, good God!

❓ WHATCHA THINKIN'? DISCUSSION QUESTIONS

1. What kinds of things are you glad God created?
2. Adam and Eve lived in a place called the Garden of Eden. Why would it have been nice to live there?
3. How can we can take care of God's creation and show him we're thankful for it?

✔ MEMORY MADNESS

Teacher's Note: Write the following verse on a chalkboard, overhead projector, or marker board. Have the class read it aloud several times. Cross out one or two words in each consecutive read-through until the children are reciting it from memory.

The Lord God placed the man in the Garden of Eden to tend and care for it. (Genesis 2:15)

CRAFTY CORNER: CREATION ON A STRING

To prepare before class:
Cut out 3" by 3" squares (or other shapes in similar sizes) of white paper. Each child will need seven squares. Cut one 6" piece of string for each child.

Supplies needed:
● paper cutouts (prepared before class)
● string (prepared before class)
● tape, glue, or a stapler
● crayons
● hole puncher

Directions:
Each child should receive seven squares. Each square corresponds to one day of creation plus the seventh day of rest. Children should draw what God created on each day. The papers can be connected together (vertically) with tape, glue, or staples. Punch a hole at the top of the paper for day 1, and loop the string through it, knotting the string. This wall hanging will remind children of the order of creation.

✜ PRAYER

Thank you, God, for creating the world, and for creating me. Help me to remember always what a good God you are.

✪ TASTY TREAT

Teacher's Note: Serve trail mix with apple juice. You can discuss how the raisins, nuts, and other parts of the mix came from the earth that God created. The apple juice came from a fruit tree—like those in the Garden of Eden.

Don't Eat from That Tree

A LESSON ABOUT CHOOSING TO OBEY

🕐 BIBLE STORY

Teacher's Note: Read to the class the story of Adam and Eve eating the fruit. It's found in Genesis 3.

🕑 THE STORY IN SONG

Teacher's Note: Play the song "Don't Eat from That Tree" from Bible Songs 1.

"DON'T EAT FROM THAT TREE"

Adam and Eve were in the Garden of Eden
Enjoying all God had made
There were all kinds of good things for eating
Life was really great
God provided everything
Then gave one small direction
Have fruit from any tree you want
With this one exception

CHORUS
God told Eve don't eat from the tree
Of the knowledge of good and evil
God said you can eat what you please
But not from that tree
Please listen to me

Along came a sneaky snake
And said the apple on that tree looks yummy
Wouldn't you like a taste?
It would feel so good in your tummy
But

REPEAT CHORUS

Eve took a bite and then she gave some to Adam
And he took a big bite too
Then they heard God walking in the garden
Calling where are you
Eve and Adam ran and hid
'Cause they were so ashamed
When you know what God wants from you
It's better to obey

And God had said don't eat from the tree
Of the knowledge of good and evil
But they did so Adam and Eve
Soon had to leave
The beautiful Garden of Eden

🕒 DIGGING DEEPER DEVOTION

Teacher's Note: Read the following devotion to the children and discuss the questions that come after it.

Have you ever wanted something so much that you did something wrong to get it? Sin often looks good. After all, no one would steal a candy bar if it didn't taste good or lie if it wouldn't get them out of trouble. But sin always catches up with you. God told Adam and Eve not to eat from one tree. But its juicy fruit looked so delicious, and it was—at least until they lost God's blessings. They found out it doesn't pay to disobey. Don't learn the hard way—stick to what's right, and you won't go wrong!

🕓 WHATCHA THINKIN'? DISCUSSION QUESTIONS

1. What was so wrong about Adam and Eve eating the fruit?
2. Why did they make their sin worse by hiding from God and blaming someone or something else?
3. Who are some people you need to obey?

🕔 MEMORY MADNESS

Teacher's Note: Write the following verse on a chalkboard, overhead projector, or marker board. Have the class read it aloud several times. Cross out one or two words in each consecutive read-through until the children are reciting it from memory.

Be careful to obey. Then all will go well with you. (Deuteronomy 6:3)

CRAFTY CORNER: PRAY TO OBEY!

To prepare before class:
On 3" by 3" squares of paper (one square per child), write the following letters (older children can write this themselves): LHMO. These letters stand for a prayer reminder—"Lord, Help Me Obey." Children can hang the finished craft on their doorknob or tape it to a mirror. Cut one 6" piece of string for each child.

Supplies needed:
- 3" by 3" squares of paper
- string
- glitter
- glue
- markers, crayons, or colored pencils
- hole puncher

Directions:
Give each child one paper square. If children are old enough, instruct them to write the following letters on their paper: LHMO. Wait to explain the meaning until craft time is over—they'll love the suspense, and their attention will be held! Direct them to decorate the paper around the letters however they want, using glitter, markers, crayons, or colored pencils. Punch a hole in the top of the paper and loop the string through it, knotting the string. Instruct them to hang their artwork on their bedroom doorknob or tape it to a mirror to remind them to pray, "Lord, Help Me Obey."

✝ PRAYER

Dear God, even when I don't feel like doing it, help me to obey you always.

🍎 TASTY TREAT

Teacher's Note: Serve gummy fruit snacks and some type of fruit punch or juice. Discuss how the fruit snacks are a reminder of the fruit that Adam and Eve ate, and that all our choices have consequences.

They Missed the Boat

A LESSON ABOUT FOLLOWING GOD INSTEAD OF THE CROWD

❶ BIBLE STORY

Teacher's Note: Read the story of Noah's ark to the class. It's found in Genesis 6:9–7:10.

❸ THE STORY IN SONG

Teacher's Note: Play the song "They Missed the Boat" from **Bible Songs 1.**

"THEY MISSED THE BOAT"

(THE RHINOPOTAMUS SONG)

The Lord told Noah
Better build a great big boat
Then look for two of every creature
That won't float
Some of the animals ran and hid
Have you ever seen a unacornipig?
Well, you won't
'Cause they missed the boat

The thunder rumbled
And lightning clapped in the sky
Then came the animals
Two of every kind
They came from dawn to dusk
But have you ever seen a rhinopotamus?
Well, you won't
'Cause they missed the boat

The rain came down
For forty days and nights
Then Noah looked around and the land
Was out of sight
He did the best any man could do
But have you ever seen an armadillgaroo?
Well, you won't
'Cause they missed the boat

Have you ever seen a bobbygoat?
Have you ever seen a katydon't?
Well, you won't
'Cause they missed the boat

❹ DIGGING DEEPER DEVOTION

Teacher's Note: Read the following devotion to the children and discuss the questions that come after it.

A rhinopotamus? You're right, there is no such thing. But there were many different creatures on the ark. In fact, everything about the Flood and the ark was different from anything anyone had ever seen. After all, no one had ever built such a ship or collected so many animals. Everyone laughed when Noah told them about God's warning to shape up or "ship out"—for real! Noah probably got tired of feeling different from everyone else. But he kept obeying God, and he didn't let others keep him from missing the boat. Be a Noah!

❷ WHATCHA THINKIN'? DISCUSSION QUESTIONS

1. People must have wondered why Noah spent so many years building a boat. What do you think they said to him?
2. During the Flood, Noah and his family were safe inside the ark. How do you suppose Noah felt about his decision to obey God then?
3. Is it sometimes hard for you to do what's right? In what situations?

❼ MEMORY MADNESS

Teacher's Note: Write the following verse on a chalkboard, overhead projector, or marker board. Have the class read it aloud several times. Cross out one or two words in each consecutive read-through until the children are reciting it from memory.

Noah did everything exactly as God had commanded him. (Genesis 6:22)

CRAFTY CORNER: THE ARK OF PROMISE

To prepare before class:
Cut paper plates in half—enough for each child to have two halves. Collect small clip-art pictures, or cut out magazine photos of animals. Make sure there are enough pictures/photos for each child to have several. These will be glued to the paper plate (ark), so they need to be small enough to fit.

Supplies needed:
● paper plates cut in half (two halves per child)
● clip art and/or photos of animals
● glue
● stapler
● crayons

Directions:
Distribute the plate halves to the students. Instruct them to either draw animals or glue the paper animals on the rounded sides of the plates (the ark). Other things they can color on their arks are a rainbow, a dove, a tree branch, or Noah and his family. Staple the two decorated halves together, creating a pocket in the middle.

Remind the children of God's promise to never again destroy the world with a flood. To help them remember God's promises and answers to prayer, they can write them on small pieces of paper and store them inside the ark.

✚ PRAYER

Dear God, thank you for always keeping your promises to me. Help me keep my promises to you, too.

✪ TASTY TREAT

Teacher's Note: Serve animal crackers, water, and maybe some colorful fruit candy to symbolize the rainbow.

Babel, Babel, Babel, Babel

A LESSON ABOUT DOING GOD'S WILL

❶ BIBLE STORY

Teacher's Note: Read the story of the Tower of Babel to the class. It's found in Genesis 11:1-9.

❷ THE STORY IN SONG

Teacher's Note: Play the song "Babel, Babel, Babel, Babel" from Bible Songs 1.

"BABEL, BABEL, BABEL, BABEL"

At first the whole world spoke one language
Everybody used the same words
The people said let's build a great city
With a tower that looks down on the birds
The Lord saw what the people were doing
And he said I don't agree with this plan
He threw them a curve
And then all they heard
Were words they didn't understand

CHORUS
Babel, Babel, Babel, Babel
What didja say?
Could you repeat yourself please?
Babel, Babel, Babel, Babel
What didja say?
It all sounds like Greek to me
Babel, Babel, Babel, Babel
Huh? What?!
Confusion everywhere
Sounds like a bunch of rabble
Took a game of Scrabble
And threw the letters up in the air

Have you got a tower you're building
Made out of boxes and jelly jars?
Or a rocket made of noodles and oatmeal
For a trip that you are planning to Mars?
Allow me please to make one suggestion
Make sure that you run it by God

'Cause when he approves
Then you can't lose
And soon it will be more than talk

REPEAT CHORUS

❸ DIGGING DEEPER DEVOTION

Teacher's Note: Read the following devotion to the children and discuss the questions that come after it.

What would you like to do when you grow up? travel the world? discover a cure for a horrible disease? train dolphins at the zoo? God wants to help you reach your goals. But first he wants you to make him number one in your life. The people who built the Tower of Babel thought they could be as wise and powerful as God; they were too proud. But God reminded them that no one is greater than he is. Make sure your plans are God's plans!

❹ WHATCHA THINKIN'? DISCUSSION QUESTIONS

1. Why were the people building the tower? Why wasn't God happy about it?
2. Have you ever done something for a bad reason? What was that reason?
3. The next time you're tempted to do something bad, what will you do to follow God's plans rather than your own?

❺ MEMORY MADNESS

Teacher's Note: Write the following verse on a chalkboard, overhead projector, or marker board. Have the class read it aloud several times. Cross out one or two words in each consecutive read-through until the children are reciting it from memory.

Pride goes before destruction, and haughtiness before a fall. (Proverbs 16:18)

CRAFTY CORNER: A TOWER OF TROUBLE

To prepare before class:
Collect empty paper towel rolls—one for each child in the class. Cut each one into eight pieces, creating eight mini rolls for each child. These will be stacked on top of each other to make a very wobbly tower.

Supplies needed:
- empty paper towel rolls
- uncooked pasta (small sizes such as macaroni)
- markers, crayons, colored pencils
- glitter
- glue

Directions:
Instruct the children to decorate each of their eight mini rolls however they want, using uncooked pasta, glitter, and any other decorative items available. When they're done, they can stack up the eight pieces of their "tower" to see how high they can build such a shaky structure. Suggest they do this again at home, possibly on a bed. Anytime they move the bed, the tower will come tumbling down—just like the Tower of Babel, which was built to bring glory to humans instead of to God.

✚ PRAYER

Dear God, help me to do what you want me to do instead of what I want to do.

TASTY TREAT

Teacher's Note: Serve dry Alpha-Bits cereal and fruit punch or juice. Talk about how the mixed-up cereal letters are like the mixed-up languages of the people God punished for building the tower.

God Specializes in Surprises
A LESSON ABOUT TRUSTING GOD TO BE GOOD

🅞 BIBLE STORY

Teacher's Note: Read the story of God's surprise for Abraham and Sarah to the class. It's found in Genesis 17:15-17, 19; 18:11-13; 21:1-7.

🅢 THE STORY IN SONG

Teacher's Note: Play the song "God Specializes in Surprises" from Bible Songs 1.

"GOD SPECIALIZES IN SURPRISES"

God appeared to Abraham at 99
And said your wife will have a son
Sarah laughed and thought that's crazy
I'm an old lady
But pretty soon she was a mum
'Cause nothing's too hard for the Lord
And you never know
What he's got in store

CHORUS
God specializes in surprises
You never know what he's gonna do
You gotta believe
'Cause he knows what you need
And he's got some good surprises for you

You might have a dream that seems impossible
And you don't even have a plan
The Father of Creation
Made your imagination
Everything is in his hands
So when things get a little rough
Keep on smiling
And don't give up

REPEAT CHORUS

You gotta believe
'Cause he knows what you need
And he's got some good surprises

You may not realize it
But he's got some good surprises for you

🅚 DIGGING DEEPER DEVOTION

Teacher's Note: Read the following devotion to the children and discuss the questions that come after it.

Imagine yourself older than old—almost 100! Wrinkles cover your face, you can't hear well anymore, and you need a cane to hobble around. Well, that's what Abraham and Sarah may have looked like when God gave them their first child. They had waited so long for a baby. It's hard to wait sometimes, but you make God proud when you trust him and are patient. Many times God's best gifts are ones he asks you to wait for. Give him time to work. He is never late, and his surprises are more wonderful than you could imagine!

🅠 WHATCHA THINKIN'? DISCUSSION QUESTIONS

1. What have you had to wait and wait . . . and wait for?
2. Why might God have wanted you to wait? Maybe to grow patience in you?
3. Can waiting for things help you trust God more? How?

🅥 MEMORY MADNESS

Teacher's Note: Write the following verse on a chalkboard, overhead projector, or marker board. Have the class read it aloud several times. Cross out one or two words in each consecutive read-through until the children are reciting it from memory.

"My thoughts . . . ," says the Lord, "are far beyond anything you could imagine." (Isaiah 55:8)

CRAFTY CORNER: CREATE-A-COUPON

To prepare before class:
Each child will need one piece of paper—any color, any size—to create a colorful coupon for one act of kindness he or she will do for a family member.

On each child's paper, print the words (in marker or on the computer):

Supplies needed:
- one piece of paper per child
- Items to decorate with:
- crayons, markers, or colored pencils
- glitter
- pictures from magazines
- scissors
- glue

Directions:
Instruct the children to think of one special act of kindness they can do to surprise someone in their family. You may want to offer a couple of suggestions to get their ideas flowing: one free chore around the house, one free back rub, one free forgiveness for a crabby day, etc. Help the younger children fill in their coupon, and instruct them to give it to someone they would like to encourage. If there's time, have the children decorate their coupons.

> SURPRISE!
> Here's a coupon for you for one free _____,
> just because you're special!
>
> To: _____
> Date: _____
> From: _____

✚ PRAYER

Dear God, you were kind to Abraham and Sarah, and you're always kind to me. Help me remember to be kind to others, too.

TASTY TREAT

Teacher's Note: Serve popcorn and juice. Discuss how popcorn begins as tiny kernels of dried corn. When those kernels are cooked—surprise! They suddenly become a delicious snack. Some of God's best gifts come in very surprising ways.

Jo-Jo-Joseph Had a Rainbow Coat

A LESSON ABOUT JEALOUSY

🄌 BIBLE STORY

Teacher's Note: Read the story of Joseph's coat to the class. It's found in Genesis 37:3-4, 18-28.

❸ THE STORY IN SONG

Teacher's Note: Play the song "Jo-Jo-Joseph Had a Rainbow Coat" from Bible Songs 1.

"JO-JO-JOSEPH HAD A RAINBOW COAT"

CHORUS
Jo-Jo-Jo
Jo-Jo-Jo
Jo-Jo-Joseph had a rainbow coat
Jo-Jo-Jo
Jo-Jo-Jo
Jo-Jo-Joseph had a rainbow coat

Did Joe's coat have green like the new grass that
  grows?
Did Joe's coat have white like flecks of falling snow?
Did Joe's coat have pink like a fluffy kitten's nose?
Did Joseph have a coat of green and white and
  pink?

REPEAT CHORUS

Did Joe's coat have orange like a carrot on your
  plate?
Did Joe's coat have purple like juice from a juicy
  grape?
Did Joe's coat have yellow like a daisy chain?
Did Joseph have a coat of orange and purple and
yellow and green and white and pink?

REPEAT CHORUS

Did Joe's coat have red like a shiny fire truck?
Did Joe's coat have brown like a squishy pool of
  mud?
Did Joe's coat have blue like the great big sky
  above?

Did Joseph have a coat of red and brown and blue
  and orange
And purple and yellow and green and white and
  pink?

REPEAT CHORUS

🄌 DIGGING DEEPER DEVOTION

Teacher's Note: Read the following devotion to the children and discuss the questions that come after it.

Joseph's brothers were so jealous! Their father gave Joseph a beautiful coat, but they got nothing. You might know what it feels like to want something someone else has. But there is a right way to behave, and Joseph's brothers chose the wrong way. Because they felt hurt, they treated Joseph very badly. Next time you feel jealous, remember that God knows everything you need. Be grateful instead for what you have. Then wait for God to fill your life with wonderful things!

🄌 WHATCHA THINKIN'? DISCUSSION QUESTIONS

1. Have you ever been jealous? If so, when?
2. How does jealousy affect how you think about or act toward someone?
3. What are some things you can be grateful for next time you feel jealous of what someone else has?

🄌 MEMORY MADNESS

Teacher's Note: Write the following verse on a chalkboard, overhead projector, or marker board. Have the class read it aloud several times. Cross out one or two words in each consecutive read-through until the children are reciting it from memory.

Love is not jealous or boastful or proud.
(1 Corinthians 13:4)

CRAFTY CORNER: A RAINBOW OF THANKS

To prepare before class:
On an 8 ½" by 11" piece of white paper, draw the outline of a coat. At the top of the page, write in bold letters: A Rainbow of Thanks! Photocopy the drawing, making one copy for each child in the class.

Supplies needed:
- photocopied drawings
- crayons, markers, or colored pencils
- pen or pencil

Directions:
During class, instruct the children to think of things and people they are thankful for. Help younger children write those on their paper coats. The coat can be colored like Joseph's coat may have looked. Tell the students that giving thanks is one way to get rid of jealousy.

✞ PRAYER

Dear God, instead of being jealous of what I don't have, remind me to give thanks for what I do have.

◔ TASTY TREAT

Teacher's Note: Serve pieces of apples, oranges, bananas, kiwi, blueberries, and purple grapes. Discuss the rainbow of colors in the fruit (red, orange, yellow, green, blue, and purple). Don't forget to give thanks for the snack!

Gideon, I'm Not Kideon

A LESSON ABOUT GOD'S STRENGTH FOR TOUGH JOBS

🕐 BIBLE STORY

Teacher's Note: Read the story of Gideon to the class. It's found in Judges 6:11-24.

🎵 THE STORY IN SONG

Teacher's Note: Play the song "Gideon, I'm Not Kideon" from Bible Songs 1.

"GIDEON, I'M NOT KIDEON"

An angel of the Lord appeared to Gideon
And said the Lord is with you
Go and save the people of Israel
And I will be with you
Gideon asked are you sure you want me?
I am the least in my family

CHORUS
Gideon, Gideon
I'm not kideon
You're the one I want for the job
Gideon, Gideon
Listen once again
This is the word of God

Jesus needs some helpers in the world today
Listening and learning
If you look you'll find so many ways
You can love by serving
If you think you're too short or too small or too thin
Remember what God told Gideon

REPEAT CHORUS

🕐 DIGGING DEEPER DEVOTION

Teacher's Note: Read the following devotion to the children and discuss the questions that come after it.

If you've ever been told to do something really hard, then you know how Gideon felt when God told him to lead a whole country! Naturally, he wasn't sure he heard correctly. God doesn't promise to give you only easy lessons to learn, but he does promise to always be with you when you follow him. He'll show you how amazing he is when you obey him—especially when it's hard.

❓ WHATCHA THINKIN'? DISCUSSION QUESTIONS

1. Why may Gideon have been scared to obey God?
2. Have you ever had to do something really hard? How did you feel?
3. What can you ask God for the next time you have to do something hard?

✓ MEMORY MADNESS

Teacher's Note: Write the following verse on a chalkboard, overhead projector, or marker board. Have the class read it aloud several times. Cross out one or two words in each consecutive read-through until the children are reciting it from memory.

Yes, the Lord has done amazing things for us! What joy! (Psalm 126:3)

CRAFTY CORNER: FAITH FLAG

To prepare before class:
Each student will need one plastic drinking straw and one 4" by 6" piece of white paper.

Supplies needed:
- plastic drinking straws
- 4" by 6" pieces of white paper
- markers, crayons, colored pencils
- small scraps of colored paper
- glitter
- paper confetti
- glue
- scissors
- tape

Directions:
On one side of each student's paper, either you or they can write the words "God is my strength!" The other side should be decorated as their own personal flag, with any type of design they choose. After their flag is decorated, tape an edge to one end of the plastic straw. Explain that just as Gideon led the Israelite army to victory, the children can be victorious, too. All they have to do is have faith in God's strength and obey him!

✚ PRAYER

Dear God, even when I'm scared help me to believe in your strength just as Gideon did.

✪ TASTY TREAT

Teacher's Note: Serve Bugles brand snacks with fruit punch or juice. Talk about how Gideon may have blown a bugle as he led God's army to victory.

Yes!

A LESSON ABOUT LISTENING FOR GOD

🕐 BIBLE STORY

Teacher's Note: Read the story of young Samuel to the class. It's found in 1 Samuel 3:1-10.

🎵 THE STORY IN SONG

Teacher's Note: Play the song "Yes!" from **Bible Songs 1.**

"YES!"

(SAMUEL'S SONG)

Samuel was sleeping, sleeping in his bed
Then a voice called out to him, Samuel it said
Samuel ran to Eli and asked what do you need?
Eli said I didn't call you
Sam go back to sleep (snore)

Samuel was sleeping, sleeping in his bed
The voice called out a second time, Samuel it said
Samuel ran to Eli and asked what do you need?
Eli said I didn't call you
Sam go back to sleep (snore)

Samuel was sleeping, sleeping in his bed
The voice called out a third time, Samuel it said
Samuel ran to Eli and asked what do you need?
Eli said it is the Lord
Answer him indeed

CHORUS
Oh, the Lord called once
The Lord called twice
The Lord called Samuel three times
Eli finally realized who was calling Sam
Sam he said
This is great
You go back to bed and wait
Next time God calls out your name
You just answer Yes!
Yes! Yes! Yes! You just answer Yes! Yes! Yes!
Yes! Yes! Yes! You just answer Yes!

Samuel was sleeping, sleeping in his bed
The voice called out the fourth time, Samuel it said
Samuel answered quickly, Yes, Lord, it is I
And kept saying yes to God
All throughout his life

REPEAT CHORUS

Samuel answered Yes!

🕐 DIGGING DEEPER DEVOTION

Teacher's Note: Read the following devotion to the children and discuss the questions that come after it.

"Yes" answers are wonderful. No one wants to be told no all the time—especially when they ask, "Can I sleep over at my friend's house?" or "Can I have my allowance?" God loves to hear yes answers from us as well. When Samuel was young, he learned to say yes to God. When God spoke, Samuel listened. God asks you a lot of questions too. When he asks you to show others his love, will you say yes? What about when he asks if you trust him? And what about when God asks if you love him? You'll definitely want to say yes!

🕐 WHATCHA THINKIN'? DISCUSSION QUESTIONS

1. Why is it so important to say yes when God or your mom and dad ask you to do something?
2. What kinds of requests do you have a hard time answering yes to? chores around the house? helping your friends or neighbors?
3. How can you be more like Samuel and obey with yes answers?

✔ MEMORY MADNESS

Teacher's Note: Write the following verse on a chalkboard, overhead projector, or marker board. Have the class read it aloud several times. Cross out one or two words in each consecutive read-through until the children are reciting it from memory.

Samuel replied, "Yes, your servant is listening." (1 Samuel 3:10)

CRAFTY CORNER: THUMBS UP FOR YES!

To prepare before class:
You will need washable, non-toxic ink and ink pads, as well as paper of a different color than the ink. Be ready with soap and water during class!

Supplies needed:
- ink pads
- washable, non-toxic ink
- paper (8 ½" by 11" is fine.)
- marker or pen

Directions:
Each student will need one piece of paper and a clean hand. Have each child make a "thumbs up" sign with their hand (a fist with the thumb sticking up). Press the hand flat (palm side down with the knuckles curled in) onto the freshly inked pad. Transfer the inked hand onto the blank paper so an impression of the "thumbs up" shows. At the top of the paper, write, "Thumbs Up for Yes Answers!"

✝ PRAYER

Dear God, help me to listen to you like Samuel did and to always say yes to whatever you want me to do.

♪ TASTY TREAT

Teacher's Note: Serve butter cookies (round with a hole in the middle) and juice. Have the kids make the thumbs-up sign, and place the cookie on their thumb to remember Samuel's thumbs-up, yes answer to God!

No Matter How Little You Are

A LESSON ABOUT BEING USED BY GOD

🛈 BIBLE STORY

Teacher's Note: Read the story of David and Goliath to the class. It's found in 1 Samuel 17.

🎵 THE STORY IN SONG

Teacher's Note: Play the song "No Matter How Little You Are" from Bible Songs 1.

"NO MATTER HOW LITTLE YOU ARE"

(YOU CAN DO BIG THINGS WITH GOD)

Goliath was a giant
Nine feet tall from toe to ear
He wore a big bronze helmet
And he waved a pointy spear
David was a young boy
With a slingshot and some stones
Though he had a mammoth problem
He knew he was not alone

CHORUS
No matter how little you are
You can do big things with God
No matter how little you are
You can do big things with God

Goliath stomped and shouted
I'll defeat this boy he roared
He looked big to all the people
But small in the eyes of the Lord
The shepherd boy stood ready
When he might have turned and fled
As Goliath moved in closer
A voice inside David said

REPEAT CHORUS

One pebble dropped Goliath
When he fell it made a thud
After being such a bully
He turned out to be a dud

So David beat that giant
And you'll beat your problem too
As long as you remember
God is always there with you

REPEAT CHORUS

🔍 DIGGING DEEPER DEVOTION

Teacher's Note: Read the following devotion to the children and discuss the questions that come after it.

Have you ever had to look way, way up to see a really tall person? Goliath was so tall that his head would probably touch the ceiling in your house! When none of the men wanted to face the giant, God sent a boy named David. Sometimes it's easy to feel small and unimportant when you're a kid. But there's something to get excited about: God's power is not limited by your age or size. When you trust him and ask him for help, God can do the impossible for you. Believe it!

❓ WHATCHA THINKIN'? DISCUSSION QUESTIONS

1. How would you feel if you were David facing the wicked giant Goliath? a little scared?
2. What are some things that make you scared?
3. Why is praying and asking God for help a great thing to do?

✔ MEMORY MADNESS

Teacher's Note: Write the following verse on a chalkboard, overhead projector, or marker board. Have the class read it aloud several times. Cross out one or two words in each consecutive read-through until the children are reciting it from memory.

I can do everything with the help of Christ who gives me the strength I need. (Philippians 4:13)

CRAFTY CORNER: ONE BIG, LITTLE SHEPHERD

Supplies needed:
- white cotton balls—several for each student
- 8 ½" by 11" white paper—one for each student
- markers, colored pencils, or crayons
- glue

Directions:
Instruct the students to glue the cotton balls relatively close together on their paper. They can draw legs and a head around each cotton ball. This is David's flock of sheep that he tended before he fought the giant Goliath. The children can draw David, Goliath, the slingshot and stones, and any other elements of the story too.

✝ PRAYER

Dear God, when I think I'm too small to do anything for you, help me to be brave like David.

🍴 TASTY TREAT

Teacher's Note: Serve a "mini-snack" of bite-sized crackers, mini-marshmallows, and small juiceboxes.

Sol, Sol the Know-It-All

A LESSON ABOUT BEING SMART AND ACTING SMART

❶ BIBLE STORY

Teacher's Note: Read the story of wise King Solomon's foolish mistakes to the class. It's found in 1 Kings 3:3-14 and 11:1-11.

❷ THE STORY IN SONG

Teacher's Note: Play the song "Sol, Sol the Know-It-All" from Bible Songs 1.

"SOL, SOL THE KNOW-IT-ALL"

King Solomon ruled Israel and wanted to serve God
So the Lord came to him in a dream and said
What do you want?
Then Solomon asked God to make him smartest in
the land
And then there wasn't anything he did not
understand

CHORUS
Oh Sol, Sol the know-it-all
Wisest man in Israel
He was smart but he took a fall
Sol, Sol the know-it-all

Sol made some great decisions, and the people
were amazed
He wrote the Proverbs proving that he was a man
of brains
He built God a holy temple in Jerusalem
Got too big for his britches, and it cost him in the
end

REPEAT CHORUS

Well, you may know a lot of things and have a lot
of stuff
But if you don't obey the Lord it still won't be
enough
So read the words of Solomon and do the things
he said

But keep your eyes on God so you don't do the
things he did

REPEAT CHORUS

❸ DIGGING DEEPER DEVOTION

Teacher's Note: Read the following devotion to the children and discuss the questions that come after it.

What is one thing you're really good at? making friends? riding a bike? getting good grades? Solomon was a very smart king a very long time ago. He knew a lot of stuff about a lot of stuff! In fact, he was wiser than everyone else. But King Solomon made some big mistakes that ruined his life. You may know a lot, but what really matters to God is whether or not your attitudes and actions please him.

❓ WHATCHA THINKIN'? DISCUSSION QUESTIONS

1. What's the difference between being smart and acting smart?
2. Which one do you think pleases God most? Why?
3. What are some smart ways to act when your parents and teachers tell you to do something?

✔ MEMORY MADNESS

Teacher's Note: Write the following verse on a chalkboard, overhead projector, or marker board. Have the class read it aloud several times. Cross out one or two words in each consecutive read-through until the children are reciting it from memory. Special note: Have younger children memorize only through "commands."

Fear God and obey his commands. . . . God will judge us for everything we do, including every secret thing, whether good or bad. (Ecclesiastes 12:13-14)

CRAFTY CORNER: KING SOLOMON'S CROWN

To prepare before class:
You'll need some lengths of classroom bulletin-board border (preferably solid color with a scalloped top edge). This border paper will become the crown, so you'll need enough to make one crown for each child's head.

Supplies needed:
- bulletin-board border paper
- stapler
- glue
- plastic "gemstones" for play
- glitter
- markers, crayons, or colored pencils
- colored tissue paper

Directions:
Fit a length of border paper around each child's head. Remove and staple the cut ends of the paper together. Instruct the children to decorate their crowns, using any of the supplies they choose.

✝ PRAYER

Dear God, help me to choose wisely and to obey what my parents and teachers tell me to do.

TASTY TREAT

Teacher's Note: Serve baby carrots, peanut butter on crackers, and juice. Discuss how healthy foods like these help them grow strong and smart like Solomon. However, they still need to ask God to help them live to please him.

Shadrach, Meshach, Abednego

A LESSON ABOUT STANDING UP FOR GOD

🔵 BIBLE STORY

Teacher's Note: Read the story of Shadrach, Meshach, and Abednego in the fiery furnace. It's found in Daniel 3.

🔵 THE STORY IN SONG

Teacher's Note: Play the song "Shadrach, Meshach, Abednego" from Bible Songs 1.

"SHADRACH, MESHACH, ABEDNEGO"

The king of Babylon built a god that was false
He told the people bow down and worship it or else
Three men wouldn't do it
The king just blew his top
He threw them in the furnace and then turned it up
    real hot

CHORUS
Shadrach, Meshach, Shadrach, Meshach,
    Abednego, Abednego
Shadrach, Meshach, Shadrach, Meshach,
    Abednego, Abednego
When things got warm
They stood by the Lord
So the king would know about the true God of
    heaven

God saw there was trouble and sent an angel
    down
Protected in the fire the men all walked around
The king said who they worship
Must really be the Lord
'Cause there were only three at first, and now I'm
    counting four

REPEAT CHORUS

🔵 DIGGING DEEPER DEVOTION

Teacher's Note: Read the following devotion to the children and discuss the questions that come after it.

Has there ever been a time when you decided to do the right thing when everyone else made the wrong choice? Shadrach, Meshach, and Abednego knew their lives could be in danger when they obeyed God instead of the king. But God protected them. Because they made the right choice, the king learned that their God was the true God. You too can make a difference by standing up for what's right. God takes care of those who love him!

🔵 WHATCHA THINKIN'? DISCUSSION QUESTIONS

1. How do you think Shadrach, Meshach, and Abednego may have felt right before they were thrown in the fiery furnace?
2. Why do you think God allowed them to be thrown in the furnace at all?
3. Have you ever decided to do the right thing even though it was hard? When was that? Did you feel good, knowing you were pleasing God?

🔵 MEMORY MADNESS

Teacher's Note: Write the following verse on a chalkboard, overhead projector, or marker board. Have the class read it aloud several times. Cross out one or two words in each consecutive read-through until the children are reciting it from memory.

The God whom we serve is able to save us.
(Daniel 3:17)

CRAFTY CORNER: THE FURNACE FLAMES

To prepare before class:
Each student will need one piece of 8 ½" by 11" paper and several 2" squares of red, orange, and yellow tissue paper.

Supplies needed:
- 8 ½" by 11" paper
- orange, yellow, and/or red tissue paper
- glue
- crayons, markers, or colored pencils

Directions:
Have each child draw what they think the furnace may have looked like. They can also draw Shadrach, Meshach, Abednego, and the angel. To add the tissue "flames," form each piece of tissue over the child's index finger, dot the tissue-tipped finger with glue, and press the tissue on their furnace drawing. The colorful "flames" will help kids visualize the fire from which God rescued Shadrach, Meshach, and Abednego.

✝ PRAYER

Dear God, sometimes it's not easy to stand up for what's right. Help me to please you even when others are against me.

🍪 TASTY TREAT

Teacher's Note: Serve cinnamon red-hot candies and water. (Crackers or pretzels can also be added to balance the sugar!) Discuss how the cinnamon candies are a reminder of the red-hot, fiery furnace from which God saved Shadrach, Meshach, and Abednego.

Meow, Meow

A LESSON ABOUT DOING WHAT'S RIGHT NO MATTER WHAT

BIBLE STORY

Teacher's Note: Read the story of Daniel in the lions' den to the class. It's found in Daniel 6.

THE STORY IN SONG

Teacher's Note: Play the song "Meow, Meow" from Bible Songs 1.

"MEOW, MEOW"

King Darius
King Darius
Made a rule that was quite nefarious
For thirty days
No one could pray
To anyone but him
Daniel went to pray
To God that same day
Not worried that he might be spied on
Because of his decree
The king said woe is me
I have thrown Daniel to the lions

CHORUS
Meow, meow
God sent his angel down
To make the lions pussycats
Meow, meow
Daniel was purrfectly fine
He didn't have a scratch

King Darius
King Darius
In the morning was quiet hystericas
He hurried down
And calling out
Said Dan are you OK?
Daniel said I'm great
The lions never ate
Not even one bite from head to sandal
The king was most relieved

And made a new decree
That all would now seek the God of Daniel

REPEAT CHORUS

DIGGING DEEPER DEVOTION

Teacher's Note: Read the following devotion to the children and discuss the questions that come after it.

Daniel worked for King Darius, but his real boss was God. So when he was told to pray to the king, he was in trouble because he prayed only to God. Because Daniel obeyed God instead of the king's wrong law, he was thrown into a den full of hungry lions. Just as God stuck by Daniel, he promises to be with you when you choose to do what's right. If God can turn the "ROAR" of a lion into a gentle "meow," he can certainly watch over you!

WHATCHA THINKIN'? DISCUSSION QUESTIONS

1. Why was King Darius's law wrong?
2. If you were Daniel, would you have felt scared to obey God instead of the king's law? Why?
3. The next time you're in trouble (and you haven't done anything wrong), how can you have faith like Daniel?

MEMORY MADNESS

Teacher's Note: Write the following verse on a chalkboard, overhead projector, or marker board. Have the class read it aloud several times. Cross out one or two words in each consecutive read-through until the children are reciting it from memory. Special note: Have younger children memorize only through "people."

The God of Daniel . . . rescues and saves his people; he performs miraculous signs and wonders in the heavens and on earth. (Daniel 6:26-27)

CRAFTY CORNER: THE "MANE" EVENT

To prepare before class:
Cut orange construction paper into 3" by ½" strips. Each student will need about a dozen strips.

Supplies needed:
- precut strips of orange construction paper
- small paper plates—one per student
- markers, colored pencils, or crayons
- glue

Directions:
Instruct the students to curl their strips of construction paper around a marker, colored pencil, or crayon, holding the paper tight for a few seconds. When the paper is released, it should hold a curly shape. Glue one end of the curled strip of paper onto the edge of the paper plate. Continue gluing these around the plate's edge. Leave space between the glued-on strips of curled paper. These spaces can be colored in. Eyes, nose, and mouth can be added to make a lion with an orange mane—similar to the lions that God kept from eating Daniel!

✝ PRAYER

Dear God, sometimes I'm scared to do what you want me to do. I'm afraid I'll get in trouble or someone will laugh at me. Help me to be brave like Daniel, knowing you're watching over me.

Teacher's Note: Either you or one of the children can say a prayer of thanks for the food and the lesson, remembering to ask God for help to what the lesson taught.

🍴 TASTY TREAT

Teacher's Note: Serve Ritz crackers with small cubes of cheese for the eyes of the lions. (Ritz are in the shape of a lion's mane.) Discuss how God saved Daniel from the fierce lions and how he came out alive!

Indigestible Jonah

A LESSON ABOUT OBEYING RIGHT AWAY

🄌 BIBLE STORY

Teacher's Note: Read the story of Jonah to the class. It's found in Jonah 1:1–3:3.

❸ THE STORY IN SONG

Teacher's Note: Play the song "Indigestible Jonah" from Bible Songs 1.

"INDIGESTIBLE JONAH"

Jonah was afraid to do what God said
So he got into a boat and sailed away instead
The ship started rockin' caught up in a storm
And Jonah wound up getting tossed overboard
Adrift in the ocean, he bobbed like a cork
Then along came a whale about the size of New
   York
Who swallowed him up
'Cause he looked so yummy to eat

Indigestible Jonah
Indigestible Jonah
Learned what mercy was about
When the whale spit him out
And went to do the will of the Lord

For three days and nights Jonah prayed to the Lord
He'd never been in a fish's belly before
He said It's cold and it's smelly, it's dark and it's wet
And I made you some promises I'll never forget
The whale grew so tired of his talkative snack
He came out of the water and threw Jonah back
hen he dried himself off and started preaching
   God's Word

Indigestible Jonah (Not yummy)
Indigestible Jonah (Not a yummy, not a yummy
   Jonah)
Learned what mercy was about
When the whale spit him out
And went to do the will of the Lord

Indigestible Jonah (Not too delicious)
Indigestible Jonah (Not so nutritious)
Learned what mercy was about
When the whale spit him out
And went to do the will of the Lord

🄌 DIGGING DEEPER DEVOTION

Teacher's Note: Read the following devotion to the children and discuss the questions that come after it.

Imagine living inside a smelly fish! Well, that's just what Jonah did. He learned a tough lesson: Disobeying is often dangerous. Fortunately for Jonah, God is merciful and saved him from a whale of a predicament! Although chances are good you won't ever be swallowed by a fish, you'll still have lots of opportunities to choose between right and wrong. Don't put yourself in danger. Obey right away, and watch God do great things for you!

❓ WHATCHA THINKIN'? DISCUSSION QUESTIONS

1. What do you think the inside of the fish looked like? Smelled like? Sounded like? Felt like?
2. Do you think Jonah may have thought he'd never get out of there? Why?
3. Have your parents ever had to give you a time-out or another punishment to help you obey them? What would have happened if you had obeyed right away?

✔ MEMORY MADNESS

Teacher's Note: Write the following verse on a chalkboard, overhead projector, or marker board. Have the class read it aloud several times. Cross out one or two words in each consecutive read-through until the children are reciting it from memory.

My salvation comes from the Lord alone.
(Jonah 2:9)

CRAFTY CORNER: A WHALE OF A TALE

To prepare before class:
Cut blue tissue paper to fit the bottom half of a piece of 8 ½" by 11" white paper. Each student will need one piece of white paper and one piece of tissue paper.

Supplies needed:
- blue tissue paper, precut
- 8 ½" by 11" white paper
- glue
- markers, colored pencils, or crayons

Directions:
Instruct the students to crinkle their tissue paper until it is full of wrinkles. Once that's done they can unfold the tissue without completely flattening out the wrinkles they just put in. Glue the edges of the tissue to the bottom half of the white paper. The wrinkles look like the waves in the sea! The kids can now add various features of the story, including the ship Jonah was tossed overboard from, the big fish, the road to Nineveh, etc.

✚ PRAYER

Dear God, when I struggle to obey, help me to obey right away!

◑ TASTY TREAT

Teacher's Note: Serve Goldfish crackers and blue Kool-Aid (for ocean water). Discuss how a big fish swallowed Jonah in the ocean and how God saved Jonah from it.

Oh-Me-Ah, Oh-My-Ah

A LESSON ABOUT STUDYING THE BIBLE

⓪ BIBLE STORY

Teacher's Note: Read about the Bible's truth to the class. Some verses to read are 2 Chronicles 20:20; Amos 3:7; Zechariah 1:6; and 2 Timothy 3:16-17.

❽ THE STORY IN SONG

Teacher's Note: Play the song "Oh-Me-Ah, Oh-My-Ah" from Bible Songs 1.

"OH-ME-AH, OH-MY-AH"

Oh-Me-Ah, Oh-My-Ah
Obadiah
He was a prophet of old and the stories he told
Were the mighty truth of the Lord

Oh-Me-Ah, Oh-My-Ah
Jeremiah
He was a prophet of old and the stories he told
Were the mighty truth of the Lord

CHORUS
All those words from long ago
Still speak to us today
The Bible's for you, and God's Word is true
Anytime and anyplace

Oh-Me-Ah, Oh-My-Ah
Zephaniah
He was a prophet of old and the stories he told
Were the mighty truth of the Lord

Oh-Me-Ah, Oh-My-Ah
Zechariah
He was a prophet of old and the stories he told
Were the mighty truth of the Lord

REPEAT CHORUS

Joel and Habakkuk
Jonah and Nahum

Amos, Micah, and Hosea
Ezekiel
Malachi
Daniel, Haggai, and Isaiah
They were the prophets of old and the stories they
 told
Were the mighty truth of the Lord
They were the prophets of old and the stories they
 told
Were the mighty truth of the Lord

Oh-Me-Ah, Oh-My-Ah, Oh-Me-Ah, Oh-My-Ah . . .

ⓦ DIGGING DEEPER DEVOTION

Teacher's Note: Read the following devotion to the children and discuss the questions that come after it.

Wouldn't it be fun to have a time machine? You could go back and visit your grandparents' grandparents or even meet Abraham Lincoln! In a way, God gave us a type of time machine when he gave us the Bible. In it are true stories of God's plans for us, of people long ago, of great wars and wonderful love stories, and of beginnings and endings. God shared many of his messages through people called prophets. Sometimes those messages told the people to behave; others told of the future. Pay attention to what God says in the Bible. It's all true, and he wrote it for you!

ⓠ WHATCHA THINKIN'? DISCUSSION QUESTIONS

1. Have you ever wondered how the Bible—such an old book—can be important today? What have you learned about the people who spoke God's Word long ago?
2. What are some important things God tells us in the Bible?
3. What's your favorite Bible story? Why?

✔ MEMORY MADNESS

*Teacher's Note: Write the following verse on a chalkboard, overhead projector, or marker board. Have the class read it aloud several times. Cross out one or two words in each consecutive read-*through until the children are reciting it from memory.

All Scripture is inspired by God and is useful to teach us what is true and to make us realize what is wrong in our lives. (2 Timothy 3:16)

CRAFTY CORNER: SHOUT IT OUT!

To prepare before class:
Students will be making megaphones to tell the world about God's truth—just as the prophets of old did (but probably without megaphones!). Each student will need one piece of construction paper—any color—precut into a triangle whose sides are all the same length. With scissors, round off two corners of each triangle so the straight edge between them is now curved.

Supplies needed:
● construction paper
● stapler
● glitter
● markers, colored pencils, or crayons
● tissue paper
● other colored paper
● glue
● scissors

Directions:
Instruct students to decorate one side of their construction paper "triangle." Once they are finished decorating, roll the triangle (decorated side out) into a cone shape, stapling one edge over the other. Explain to the kids that they now have a megaphone to help them tell the world about the wonderful messages of God's truth and love!

✚ PRAYER

Dear God, as one of your children, I want to tell the world about you. Give me the right words to say so other people will want to know you, too.

♫ TASTY TREAT

Teacher's Note: Serve soda crackers and grape punch. Discuss how the prophets spoke God's truth about life and about the Messiah—Jesus. This snack is like a communion dinner symbolizing Jesus' death and resurrection, of which the prophets spoke.